The Wonderful Surprise

by Martha Marshall
illustrated by
James Conaway

Published by The Dandelion House
A Division of The Child's World

for distribution by VICTOR
BOOKS a division of SP Publications, Inc.
WHEATON. ILLINOIS 60187

Offices also in
Whitby, Ontario, Canada
Amersham-on-the-Hill, Bucks, England

Published by The Dandelion House, A Division of The Child's World, Inc.
© 1983 SP Publications, Inc. All rights reserved. Printed in U.S.A.

A Book for Early Readers.

Library of Congress Cataloging in Publication Data

Marshall, Martha, 1926-
  The wonderful surprise.

  Summary: Tells how Jesus rose from the dead and
appeared first to Mary Magdalene and later to others
among his followers and friends.
    1. Jesus Christ—Resurrection—Juvenile literature.
2. Jesus Christ—Appearances—Juvenile literature.
[1. Jesus Christ—Resurrection.   2. Easter.   3. Bible
stories—N.T.]   I. Conaway, James, 1944-   ill.
II. Title.
BT481.M347   1983   232'.5   83-7343
ISBN 0-89693-214-1

1 2 3 4 5 6 7 8 9 10 11 12 R 90 89 88 87 86 85 84 83

The Wonderful Surprise

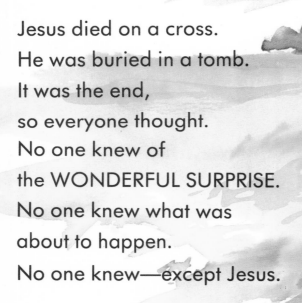

Jesus died on a cross.
He was buried in a tomb.
It was the end,
so everyone thought.
No one knew of
the WONDERFUL SURPRISE.
No one knew what was
about to happen.
No one knew—except Jesus.

Jesus knew.
He had known all along.
He had told His friends.
But they had not understood.

The WONDERFUL SURPRISE happened
just as Jesus had known it would!
It happened very early in the morning
on the first day of the week.

Jesus arose from the dead!
He was alive!
Jesus was alive!

The soldiers who had been at the tomb
did not know that Jesus was alive.
They only knew that the tomb was empty.
But Mary Magdalene knew!
For early in the morning,
she had stood by the tomb, crying.
A man stood close to her.
The man said, "Why are you crying?"

Mary Magdalene thought He was the gardener.
But when He said, "Mary,"
Mary knew who He was!
"MY MASTER!" she cried happily.

Jesus was alive!
Mary Magdalene knew.
For she had seen Him!

The temple leaders did not know
Jesus was alive.
King Herod did not know
Jesus was alive.

But some women knew!
For early that morning
the women had gone to the tomb.
Jesus was not there.
Two angels were there.
The angels said,
"He is not here. He is alive.
Hurry and tell His friends."
The women hurried away.

Suddenly Jesus met them.
"Greetings," He said.
The women fell down before Him,
touching His feet.

Jesus was alive.
The women knew.
For they had seen Him!
They had touched Him!

15

Most people in the town of Emmaus
did not know Jesus was alive.
But two men knew.

The two men walked to Emmaus.
They were sad.
Jesus of Nazareth had died on a cross.
The two talked about this as they walked.

Suddenly Jesus came
and walked with them.
At first they did not know Him.

But when they stopped to eat,
they knew He was Jesus!

Jesus was alive.
The two men knew.
For they had walked with Him.
They had eaten with Him.

19

Most of the fishermen from Galilee
did not know Jesus was alive.

But Peter knew.
Peter and his friend, John,
had run to the tomb.

21

Peter went inside and looked around.
He saw that the tomb was empty.

Later that day, Jesus stood before him!
Then Peter knew that Jesus
had risen from the dead.

Jesus was alive!
Peter knew.
For he had seen Him!
He had talked with Him!

Most of the people in Jerusalem
did not know that Jesus was alive.
But ten of Jesus' helpers knew!
The ten had been in a room in Jerusalem.

As they talked, Jesus stood among them!
He spoke to them.
He showed them the nail scars in His hands.
He showed them the scar in His side.
He ate with them.

The ten were so happy!
Jesus had come back to them.
Jesus was alive!
The ten disciples knew!

For they had seen Him!
They had eaten with Him!

On that first day of the week long ago,
only a few people knew that Jesus was alive.
But soon over 500 people knew!

Jesus and His special helpers
went to a mountain in Galilee.
Over 500 people were there with them.
Jesus told them to
tell others all about Him.
"Tell people here and everywhere,"
Jesus said.

Jesus was alive!
Over 500 knew.
For they had seen Him.
They had heard Him!

Many people today do not know that Jesus lives!
But we know!
We have not seen Him,
or touched Him,
or heard Him speak,
as did His friends long ago.

But we have the Bible.
It tells us that Jesus lives!
And we believe!

"Blessed are those who haven't seen me and believe anyway." —John 20:29b (TLB)